A River Beyond

Michael Piper

Acknowledgments

~ I would like to thank the enormous help given to me in creating this story. For their input, their guidance, and their editing, I wish to thank Dave Piper, Dave White, Ruth Brick, Bradey Day, Jennifer Kostelecky and my wife, Ashley. Also, special thanks to Patti Piper, who was with me every step of the way.

A

River

Beyond

~ For my parents. May I love as you have loved.

Absolute Silence leads to Sadness. It is the image of Death.
~Jean Jacques Rousseau

Chapter One

The sadness took my voice. It was that simple. Why was that so hard to understand? Everyone kept trying and this shrink was no different.

So here I was, stuck in my own personal hell. I knew I had serious problems and I knew that Dr. Robbins, my counselor, couldn't help. My aunt thought otherwise, convinced that I would speak again, convinced that maybe if I kept meeting with Dr. Robbins, somehow things would get better. She was nice enough, and she meant well, but there was nothing that could undo the past; my state was permanent, my only cure would be death. Perhaps my aunt knew, knew of this suicidal fantasy. Perhaps, that knowledge is what led me here to Dr. Robbins. Regardless, here I was, stuck on her couch, being asked to do the impossible. Being asked to move on and forget.

"Have you thought about the crash?" Dr. Robbins asked as she handed me a pencil and a pad of paper. Her room was cozy with special certificates covering the walls. *How much money my aunt has paid for all these sessions*, I thought.

This was my weekly meeting with Dr. Robbins and the routine had become very predictable. Since I couldn't talk, the conversation was limited. She would offer advice, she would read to me from different books, and she would always try to get me to communicate. The pad and pencil were not a new trick.

"David, maybe you could write a few words…or maybe even just one word…when you think about the crash, what word comes to mind?" Dr. Robbins pressed.

2

This was insulting. Write a word about the crash. While I had become an expert on hiding my emotions, underneath I felt the swell. My heart raced and my eyes held back the flood-gate of tears. My stomach wrenched and my breathing became difficult. Suffocating, I thought back to that night.

We were leaving a restaurant in Seattle, my parents and I. We were out celebrating that my mom was pregnant and that we learned the sex of the baby. My parents had secretly hoped for a girl since they already had a boy in me; and a girl it was. As we ate dinner, we spent the whole time talking about names and dreaming about the future. Despite how close I was to my parents, I was excited to share them with my sister. I was a freshman in high school, so besides being a big brother I could be like a parent, too.

We left the restaurant with smiles and hugs and began our drive home. Then we pulled up to an intersection and life ended. We were waiting at a red light and I remember a quick slam of metal and blurred vision. I woke up to the moans of my parents. I unbuckled myself from my seatbelt and crawled out of the car…sirens got louder. Then I saw the front of my parents four-door Tahoe, the part of the vehicle that took the worst of the blow. It was crumpled like tinfoil.

I got up and gravitated towards the groans. My parents were alive, covered in blood and glass. I tried to open what was left of the door to get them out; I can't remember much after that.

November 13, 2009. My parents murdered, killed in a car crash. A drunk driver ran through a red light. The police officer said that all four died on impact, even though I knew better; I remembered their pain. My mom, my dad, my unborn sister, and some drunken idiot all destroyed; life taken away in an instant.

While I didn't realize it right away, god also died in the crash. I secretly had my doubts all along. I saw no evidence of god in this world and the things people told me about god seemed to contradict the very idea of such a being. The bible (which claimed to be the word of god) was weird, full of contradictions and at times downright evil. My doubts became the truth that night. An all-loving, all-powerful god would have intervened. Everything I loved and everything I thought I loved was destroyed, including god.

"You can write anything you feel, David," Dr. Robbin's clinical voice snapped me back from the daydream. I took the pencil and broke it in two. Dr. Robbins gave me a smile of compassion. If she was disappointed she did not show it. *That's why they pay her the big bucks.*

Dr. Robbins spent the rest of our time reading some "helpful stuff" to me. When it was over my aunt was quietly waiting in the lobby. She and the doctor talked for a little while and then we headed home. In the car I thought about the crash and how my life got to this point.

After the crash and the hospital, things moved pretty fast. There was a funeral and people I barely even knew offered their support. Everyone cried except me. Then I was sent up north to a town in Washington called Bellingham. My aunt was my dad's sister and lived with my uncle in Bellingham; they would be my guardians now according to the "will." Once I got there, life slowed to a stop and I began to rot. It rained for months without stopping...and somewhere in that midst, in that sadness, I lost my voice. I can't remember the exact day, but my voice withdrew from life and I could no longer speak. It was as simple and cold as that.

My aunt worried and worried. She said that I needed to "talk," that I needed to "cry"...she said that holding everything in like this was going to destroy me. It wasn't like I planned this reaction...it wasn't like I wanted this...it wasn't like I wanted to destroy myself. I just plain couldn't speak. All the adults thought I was "ill"; they were probably right.

Not speaking didn't help things at my new school. I was a freshman and the move to a new high school was unsuccessful for a mute like me. Some people made fun of me and others just avoided. Some didn't know what to do...neither did the teachers.

4

In January, we had a big meeting after school. It was me, my aunt, my uncle, some teachers and my counselor (all together to discuss how weird I was). They all talked and offered suggestions and then all told me how much they cared, how sorry they were. None of this helped. I sat there and told myself to talk; I couldn't. The next day my aunt withdrew me from school. In her words "I was going to take the year off, I was going to see a specialist and get my mind right;" which is what brought me here to Dr. Robbins.

So there I was. I spent my days alone, listening to my i-Pod. Once a week I saw a shrink. At night I lay awake, afraid to fall asleep. When I did, it was bad.

Most of my dreams were nightmares. Often I would see my parents, covered in blood and screaming in pain...sometimes I would see my baby sister, too...crying and dying. Every once in a while I would dream of revenge. Just the drunk driver, myself and a baseball bat. Thoughts of hurting him were the only comfort in my closed world, but he was dead, too. Awake, I just stared at walls and listened to my music. My thoughts were dark. No wonder my aunt was so scared.

My mental state was probably too much for my aunt. I couldn't blame her. My uncle and she seemed to quietly fight more and more and I wondered what role I played in that. They were almost as silent as me by the time June rolled around.

I really was trying...I really wanted to talk. I couldn't and that made it even worse. There was no solution, no hope for myself or those I was hurting. Without a solution the reality of what I needed to do set in. That is when I really started to think about it; when it really became a viable option. I could kill myself...it sounded like a good idea. I wouldn't be a burden to my aunt anymore and I had nothing to live for...why not? The pain would end and it would all be over. No more struggle to talk, no more disappointment, no more memories of the crash, no more pain. I wondered what would happen when I died. Would I go to heaven? Hell? Or would I just disappear? Probably just disappear...after all, there was no god.

Maybe my aunt sensed my thoughts. Maybe she just needed a break. Whatever the reason, my thoughts of suicide were postponed. After my latest session with Dr. Robbins, I went to my room, where I spent the rest of the night. The next day I got the news. It was late morning when she told me. I was in the kitchen staring out the window as my cereal became soggy.

"David, baby," my aunt grabbed my chin so she could turn my face, so we could make eye contact. Her eyes were red; she looked horrible...tired. I knew it was my fault.

"Davey, I have made a decision...it has been seven months now," she paused to compose herself. "I can't help you and you aren't getting better...in fact, I think you are getting worse."

I felt sad but no tears could form. I wanted to tell her I was sorry, but I couldn't speak. I responded like I always did...a blank stare of distant eyes.

"I spoke with your grandma; she is going to take you in for the summer...maybe longer...tomorrow we will make the drive...okay hon." My aunt moved forward and gave me a kiss on the forehead. She then got up and left me alone in the kitchen. I stared outside at the grey sky as my cereal turned to complete mush.

I thought about this. I would go. I wouldn't kill myself quite yet. My grandma lived in Ennis, Montana. I wanted for one last time to fish the waters I fished so many times with my dad. It was there in Ennis that I learned of family. Ennis held the story of my family and all that I lost. It would be a fitting place to die.

Eventually, all things merge into one, and a river runs through it. The river was cut by the world's great flood and runs over rocks from the basement of time. On some of the rocks are timeless raindrops. Under the rocks are the words, and some of the words are theirs. I am haunted by waters.
~*Norman Fitzroy A River Runs Through It*

9

Chapter Two

We left Bellingham early the next morning. It was still dark outside and I could see the moon. It was big and bright, lighting the way as my aunt's two-door Toyota Camry pulled out of the driveway and away from Bellingham. The aroma of her coffee filled the car. Our 12-hour journey was underway.

I rested my head on the window and stared at the painted lines of the interstate. My i-Pod was my comfort, my safe place. I immediately put on my headphones and I listened to my music as I thought about car wrecks. We were going pretty fast right now...what if a drunk driver hit us? I wanted to die but I didn't want my aunt to. She had done a lot for me...I was sorry that I had put so much on her and I wished that my brain was different...that I could cry...that I could handle my parents death...that I was normal. I didn't want this...I began to fanaticize about bashing the drunk driver's head with my baseball bat; I felt a little better with the thought.

Soon we were traveling over the Cascade Mountains on Interstate-90. The big green trees covered the landscape and engulfed my aunt's little car. The clouds were touching the trees and a wet Washington mist consumed the air. Soon we would be over the mountain range and into Eastern Washington, a much drier climate. I had definitely had enough of the sogginess and was glad to depart the moisture.

Five hours into the drive and my aunt hadn't said a word. Even though I couldn't speak, she was always talking to me. I wondered what she was thinking about...I was sure that she was

10

glad to be getting rid of me. I took my i-Pod off as we rolled into the desert topography of Eastern Washington. The sun touched my face through the window and a feeling of warmth came over me. It felt good.

My aunt was listening to some worship music. I never cared for the stuff. People singing and praising a god who never shows himself, a god who wants your money, a god who if you don't follow his ways will send you to an eternity of hell, a god that can't protect you or your loved ones. It was obvious to me that this god was a sham and that people who believed in this system, this dogma, were blind. My poor aunt still did, in spite of all the evidence, in spite of the fact that she was driving her mute nephew to Montana because she couldn't help him cope with the death of her brother and his pregnant wife. There was no god.

The desert of Eastern Washington turned green as we approached the Rocky Mountains. In Spokane we stopped for gas and lunch. Not long after that we were in Idaho. Again massive trees filled the landscape. We were halfway to Grandma's house. I wondered what she would think of me now. Last time I saw her was at my parents' funeral...I was still able to talk a little then...I wasn't a total freak yet.

"Davey baby," my aunt's voice broke my train of thought, "Davey, I love you...can you listen to me?"

I turned my head and looked at my aunt. Her tired face stared out at the road. Her hands clutched the steering wheel. Her eyes deep with concern and thought...contemplating her words.

"I want you to know that you can come back to Bellingham anytime...it's not like we are kicking you out." She paused to stop herself from crying. "It's just that I think your grandma might be able to help more than I can...your uncle and I are having a lot of problems, not that our marriage is an excuse...we just thought that maybe Ennis would be a better place for you right now...but if we are wrong you just come right back...ok...I love you David...I promised your dad that I would

11

take care of you...sending you to Ennis might not seem like it but I am trying to do that..."

I loved my aunt. My parents would have been happy with her efforts to restore my life. I wished I could tell her that everything was going to be ok. But everything wasn't. This trip was only going to delay the inevitable. I wasn't going to find my voice. My life was over. I wasn't sure when, but my suicide was right around the corner. Soon I would join my parents and disappear into nothingness.

My aunt tried to hold back her tears but her eyes watered the rest of the way to Ennis. Her Camry weaved and rounded the path outlined by the lonely Montana interstate. The smell of fresh pines crept in through the windows. Passing through Missoula the Blackfoot River swayed back and forth. I closed my eyes and imagined the fish. Then it was through the city of Butte, a rundown mining town, and onward towards Ennis.

The highway soon linked up with the Jefferson River, which meant we were close. The Jefferson would join the Gallatin and the Madison as the three tributaries which make up the mighty Missouri River.

The Madison runs through Ennis and has a deep history with my family. This was the river I first learned to fish on when I was a little boy...and not spinner fishing like some hack. True fishing. Fly-fishing. My father and my grandpa taught me how to fly-fish on this very water. Looking at the current I saw my family and I was reminded of how alone I was.

A grandma is a little bit parent, a little bit teacher, and a little bit best friend.
~Unknown

Chapter Three

Ennis is a small town. Only about 900 people live here full time and that was too small for my parents. My dad's career brought the Tucker family to Seattle when I was in third grade. My mom, my dad, and I, all loaded up the van and headed west…but we always looked back. Even though we left Montana, it never really left us. I still considered myself "from Montana" even if I had lived in Seattle for the last five years. Every summer we vacationed here and I knew the waters and the mountains as good as any local. My parents decided to leave for a better opportunity and so I could "grow." Now here I was returning to the place that supposedly was stunting my growth as a shell of the person who left. *Irony is cruel.*

No sooner had we entered Ennis than my aunt's car pulled up to grandma and grandpa's house. Grandpa Tucker passed away two years ago so I guess it was just Grandma's house now, but I still considered it "theirs." It was a little yellow one-story home. Three bedrooms, one kitchen and a back porch fit for *Sunset* magazine. The Madison River was just a stone's throw from the porch as the waters flowed peacefully by the property. Grandma's house was only a mile from downtown Ennis but it felt worlds away from civilization. It was just a little yellow house and a river, but it held all the history of my family.

My grandma was sitting by the living room window which faced the road as we pulled in, waiting for our arrival. She hustled out to help as we unloaded the car. My aunt burst into tears as grandma walked out and they embraced. I stood awkwardly holding my bags waiting for the exchange to end. My grandma just kept telling her that everything was going to be alright. Their embrace ended and then my aunt and grandma turned towards me.

Grandma looked me up and down and said, "Well hello to you too, Davey. How about you stop chattering for a moment a give your grandma a big hug?"

She threw her arms wide open and I walked into a great big grandma bear hug.

"I love you David, I love you so much," she whispered.

Then the three of us headed inside. I placed my stuff in my dad's old bedroom…the room he lived in as a kid and the room I always slept in when we visited. I sat down on the bed and felt the darkness surround me again. I had never been in this house or in this town without them. I missed my parents so much.

"Hope you two brought your appetites!" My grandma called from the kitchen. "I made your favorites; tonight we celebrate!"

"Celebrate what, Mom?" I heard my aunt ask from the kitchen as well. Her voice was clearly annoyed and pessimistic.

I got up from the bed and headed towards the conversation. *Yeah, celebrate what?*

"Celebrate the fact that my beautiful daughter is here, that Davey has come back to Ennis, and that an old lady has company, of course!" Grandma explained.

"Mom, really…" my aunt rolled her eyes and then stopped mid-sentence. We didn't agree with grandma but who could argue with her? She might just be the single most wonderful person in the world.

Dinner was a feast. I tried to eat as much as I could but my condition never gave me much of an appetite. Still I tried…I didn't want to disappoint, even though I knew I was way past that. I ate half a scoop of mashed potatoes, some of my salad and two bites of the roast and that was it…the most food I had consumed in a single sitting since the crash.

"Well Ma," my aunt looked at my plate, "looks like you're already having a good effect on our boy." My aunt smiled at me and winked.

"Well, there is more where that came from, David," my grandma looked at me, "we need to fatten you up a bit...you're way too skinny you know." She shook her finger in my direction.

I sat and stared at my plate for a few more minutes and then my grandma excused me from the table. I took my plate over to the sink, and then slid to my room. I put my headphones back on and fell into deep thought. I wondered what my life would be like if the crash never happened. I wondered how long I would make it before I killed myself. I had hoped that maybe I would feel better being in Ennis. I didn't.

Over my music, I could hear them cleaning up the dishes and then settling in the living room. I turned my music off so I could hear the conversation. The living room shared a wall with my dad's room...even though my door was closed I could make out the words.

"So never even a peep, huh?" Grandma's voice questioned.

"Nothing Ma...I mean he listens...like tonight over dinner...and he does what he is told...he just never talks...never does much besides mope...mope and listen to music," my aunt was obviously talking about me, the freak.

"Well, it's not your fault, Honey."

"It feels like it, Ma...I failed...I failed as a guardian...I failed as a wife...I've failed God" my aunt's voice trembled.

"Now you listen to me, Dear," my grandma's voice got loud and serious. "David's got some serious stuff to work through...stuff that is on him and no one else...you loved and that is all you can do...and your husband failed you. Don't you forget that...and you can't fail God, Sweetheart, God doesn't work like that."

Listening to the conversation just added to my misery. I began to worry. I had ruined my aunt's life...what would stop

18

me from ruining my grandma's? Death needed to come soon. I needed to stop hurting and I needed to stop hurting others.

I heard tears and hugs and I put my headphones back on. I was alone. Nothing could save me, not even Grandma Tucker.

Slowly I faded away into a slumber. Somewhere between the conscious and unconscious world I heard a voice. Loud and clear I heard a voice, my dad's voice.

"Hang in there, *Champ*," he said.

I sprang up in my bed and re-entered the conscious world. What the heck was that? My thoughts, my imagination must have produced the fantasy. But it felt so good to hear that I silently waited and hoped that it would happen again. It didn't and it took a long time to fall back asleep.

Darkness. Imprisoning me. All that I see. Absolute horror. I cannot live. I cannot die. Trapped in myself. My body my holding cell.
~Metallica "One"

Chapter Four

The next morning I awoke remembering my hallucination from last night. I had forgotten how my dad used to always call me *Champ*. I had forgotten the tone and specific sound of his voice. Last night brought those memories back and with those memories more pain. I stayed in bed staring at the ceiling thinking about all of this. I could hear my grandma and aunt talking and moving throughout the house. Then a knock on my door.

"David…I'm coming in, sweetie." My aunt opened the door as she spoke.

She came in, looked me in the eye, paused, and then walked towards the bed. She sat down right next to me and began running her hand though my hair. She was all dressed and had her purse over her shoulder. This was goodbye.

"Hey, Kiddo," she smiled. "I need a big favor from you…okay?"

I just stared back and listened.

"I need you to do two things. Take care of grandma…she's getting old…okay?" My aunt voice's was really serious and demanding… "and the most important thing… listen… you need to find whatever it is you need…we need you back, Davey."

She stopped speaking and leaned down for a big hug. I felt wet tears drop on my shoulder. I waited for the hug to end.

"Sorry I couldn't help, David." My aunt got up and exited the room closing the door behind her. I heard mumbled conversation and then the Camry fired up outside. The sounds of the car pulled out of the driveway as I stared at the ceiling again.

I didn't move for an hour or two and then my door opened again. No knock. It was Grandma. She took two steps inside and then started in.

"Get up, Davey…it's beautiful outside and you're wasting it. Take a shower. When you're done I got breakfast for ya." She threw a towel and it landed on my face. I didn't move.

"Now!" she yelled.

I listened and got up. After my shower I sat down for breakfast; my grandma was sitting at the table waiting for me. I only took down half a piece of toast and a little of the scrambled eggs. My grandma wasn't happy with my effort but only gave me a little grief. She had bigger issues with me than my caloric intake.

"Alright, Buddy, it's time to talk about how things are gonna work here." Her voice demanded my respect. "Look me in the eye, David."

I looked up from my half-eaten breakfast. My grandma's older age was apparent as I looked at her. I hadn't really noticed it yesterday, but she looked much older than the grandma of my childhood. *So much has changed*, I thought.

"Now, I ain't gonna kid you, Buddy," my grandma began. "You have been dealt a horrible hand…losing your mom and dad like that…just cause of some drunk fool; you and I both know it makes no sense. You got every right to be mad, you got every right to be blue…I ain't gonna hassle you about that, ok."

My grandma stopped to think. I looked back down at my plate. Her voice started again.

"I ain't gonna pretend I know what's going on in your head…I don't understand the whole not talking thing, but if that's how you want it to be…who am I to try to change you?...Besides sometimes words are just way too overrated anyways…Lord knows I did some crazy stuff when I lost your

23

grandpa." My grandma stopped to chuckle. I stared at my crusting breakfast.

"But, here is how things are gonna go around here. I am gonna kick you out of my house."

I looked up from my plate. She had my attention...this I didn't expect.

"Yep, you aren't allowed inside from after breakfast until dinner. I sure as hell don't have the answer for you, Davey...but this river, these mountains, they do...Listen to them, talk to them if you can...Yep, that's what you're gonna do, and there are no ifs, ands, or buts about it." My grandma seemed proud of her plan.

Then she continued, "I got a sack lunch waiting for you right next to your papa's fishing gear, out on the back porch. Your fishing stuff is gone...your dad's gear will have to do." My grandma pointed out back.

"Now scram," my grandma got up and started to clean the table.

"Dinner's at five; I got us some steaks...love you, Grandson."

I followed my grandma's orders and headed outside. On the back porch was a sack lunch, just like she said, with a big heart drawn on the paper bag. Next to it my dad's fishing gear. His green fly-rod, his brown fishing vest, his tan fishing bag all sitting there. My dad's gear waiting for use. If I could cry, this moment certainly would have been the time.

I picked up his stuff. I could smell the aroma of dried trout slime on the fishing bag as I threw it around my shoulder. The vest fit perfectly, like it was made for me. The pole was ready to go, already put together with a brown mosquito dry fly, tied on and ready for casting. I walked away from grandma's house and towards the Madison.

The stretch of the Madison that runs through Ennis is called the *Fifty Mile Riffle*, a slow peaceful stretch that runs from Quake Lake to the Ennis Lake Dam. This section of river is a wide peaceful flow. No rapids, no boulders, open valley, grass-lined banks guiding the quiet river through the beautiful Madison valley. Perfect conditions for dry-flies. Conditions that only an experienced fly-fisherman can truly appreciate.

As I walked towards the river I remembered the magic of fishing. Fishing somehow had the power to connect me to this earth, my family and my soul. I approached the water and then walked downstream for about a mile; I wanted to begin at our usual drop-in spot. I wasn't wearing any waders and the shallows up ahead were perfect for knee-deep fishing. Three summers ago my dad caught a 26-inch brown trout, right at that very spot. My mom said that she could hear my father, my grandpa and me hollering all the way from grandma's as he pulled in the fish. That was the last summer all three of us fished the Madison together. My grandpa passed away soon thereafter, and now my dad as well. It was just me now.

I walked up to our usual drop-in spot. The thought of fishing this very location was the only thing I had to look forward to in this life. And there I stood, frozen. I couldn't fish these waters. Fishing was the most intimate thing my father and I shared…fishing without him didn't seem right. So I stopped, I couldn't go on without him. I just sat there for hours and watched the water run by. I saw countless fish jump; I saw several drift boats pass by. Fishing was all around me and I couldn't get myself to get in the water. Just like talking, I was paralyzed. The David I knew, the David before the crash would have caught the day's limit by now. The person I now was, this person who couldn't talk, who couldn't cry, who couldn't fish, this person wasn't me. My grandma said this valley had the answers. Her intentions were good but I doubted that any answers were to be found. Only reminders of a life that was gone.

The day passed by slowly and painfully. I ate a little of the lunch and threw the rest in the river…*if I wasn't going to fish at least I could feed them,* I thought. There was a large rock that I spent most of the day sitting on. I began to plan the best way to kill myself. I wondered how I could do this without hurting my

25

grandma…I figured that I couldn't do it without hurting her in some way, but I reasoned that taking care of me was going to hurt even more. People say suicide is selfish and I agreed, but I had no other option. Those people don't understand true pain anyway.

I waited until my watch read 4:45 before I headed back. Just like my grandma asked, I wouldn't go back until dinner time. I walked back to the house and up to the back porch and placed my father's fishing gear on the porch, in the same spot my grandma had chosen. The aroma of meat filled the air.

"Davey-boy!" My grandma clapped her hands as she opened the back door to greet me. She threw her arms around me and squeezed.

Then she walked over to my dad's fishing bag and opened it up, inspecting the contents. She placed the bone-dry bag down and placed her hands on her side.

"Huh," she paused, "David, baby, you better start catching some fish…your grandma ain't rich and we can't eat steak every night."

I just stared into space, a little ashamed. She knew what I was up to today.

"Ok," she clapped, "get inside…steaks are ready!"

I was able to eat a fair amount again and I hoped in my grandma's eyes that would make up for the lack of fishing earlier. After dinner we cleaned up and headed to the living room. I listened to my i-Pod and my grandma read as the sun disappeared and night set in. I ended the day making plans for my suicide. I decided that slitting my wrists by the river would be the easiest and most effective method.

*Amazing Grace, how sweet the sound, that saved a wretch like
me.
~John Newton*

Chapter Five

The next morning was the same routine. Grandma forced me out of bed, fed me breakfast, and then kicked me out. I grabbed my dad's gear, the sack lunch and I headed out.

As I was walking downriver, a drift boat passed by. In the boat were two fishermen, floating peacefully and casting with perfection. This boat caught my attention because it looked just like grandpa's old drift boat. It had a bright red paint job with a yellow stripe across the top, just like grandpa's. Even more interesting, the two men in the boat reminded me very much of my father and my grandpa. They were on the other side of the river, too far away for me to make out their faces, but I stopped and watched...pretending it was them.

Then the guy who looked like my dad stopped fishing to look my way. He started yelling in my direction. Was the man yelling at me? It looked like it. What was he saying? I couldn't understand. I watched as the man placed his hands around his mouth to direct his voice my way. Yes, it was obvious this guy was yelling at me. They had floated a good distance now and I could barely make out the last thing he said.

"What are you waiting for champ?" The stranger's voice made its way to me over the sound of the current.

I stood frozen. Scared. Goose bumps lifted up on my arm. *Crazy*, I thought. *Couldn't be real...just couldn't be...and if it was, probably just a coincidence.*

I walked downriver towards our starting spot convincing myself that the men in the drift boat were a couple of strangers, and what I heard was either a weird coincidence, or just a manufactured fantasy in my mind. Either way, my dad was dead.

But as I continued to stroll down the river, I did decide one thing. *Yeah, what was I waiting for? Today I would fish!*

I arrived at the entry spot. It was early afternoon and the sun was starting to warm my exposed skin. Right by the river was the large rock that I spent yesterday sitting on. I sat down again on the familiar stone and prepared my gear. I smeared floatant gel on the mosquito and I checked the pole's alignment, then I stood up, placed my lunch on the rock and walked towards the water. I stood tall for a moment, analyzing the current...preparing my next move. Then I stepped into the water.

The ice over my heart seemed to lift slightly as the cold water ran over my feet. I walked further out as the river made its way to my knees...a cool chill rushed through my body. I wasted no time and began letting out my line. A soft breeze moved through the air and the ripples methodically sang their song. This feeling, the feeling of fishing was ingrained in my blood; I had forgotten how good it felt.

Whoosh, Whooosh, Whooosh, Whoooosh, the sound of my fly traveling through the air lengthened as I let out more and more line. My father's instruction on how to cast ran through my mind...*ten and two, Son, ten and two.* My eye spied a perfect ripple pool...a perfect landing spot for my fly...a perfect place for a hungry trout. I hadn't missed a beat. Raised as a Tucker I was a true fisherman...my fly landed softly in the swirling pool...as naturally and as unsuspecting as a real mosquito.

The fly moved with the water for only a few seconds. Then the rush, the unexplainable feeling that only a fisherman can understand entered my chest. *BAM!* My first cast landed a fish...the fish was strong and she immediately fought, pulling my line out of the reel...I loosened the drag and let her have it...I didn't want to lose this one...the joy of bringing her in was underway.

It didn't take long for me to realize that this wasn't your ordinary river trout. This fish was a monster. She jumped once during the battle and I couldn't believe my eyes…probably over 20 inches…maybe the size of the one my dad caught on this very stretch.

I was unprepared. I didn't have waders and more importantly I didn't have a net. If I wanted to bring this fish in I needed to tire her out…I stripped out more line for her to run with. Then I began to reel only when I felt no tension…when she pulled I let her; I just wanted to keep the line tight. I began making my way back to shore…trying to find an easy place to lift her out of the water once I had her reeled in. And, in that moment, the fish found her freedom.

The rocks which lie under the majestic river can be as slippery as an ice rink. In my haste, I stepped without securing myself. My whole body fell into the water and I dropped my dad's pole. I quickly scrambled and was able to grab the rod…I found my footing and stood back up, soaked from head to toe. During that time there was no tension on the line, a perfect opportunity for a smart fish to spit the hook. She did…I reeled, but felt no fish…She was gone.

I cursed myself and began to reel in the slack. Then my line completely halted. It was stuck, and stuck well. A wise fisherman would have a good chance of freeing his line in these conditions. My fly was probably snagged on an underwater branch or maybe lodged under a rock. I just needed to find the right angle to free my line. Instead, mad that I just lost a prize fish, I jerked. I jerked my line with everything I had. Sure enough, it snapped.

I walked back to the riverbank in total defeat. My line was broken, I lost my fish and I was much wetter than intended. My feet touched dry land. *At least you're fishing.*

I began the tedious work of re-rigging my line. I really made a good mess…in addition to a new fly I was going to need a brand new leader. I got it out from my dad's vest and began the work.

My father was a wonderful teacher, but if he had a flaw, it was this. He always took over for me when things got too difficult, and tying a nail knot was the most difficult knot for fly-fishing. Yes, there were easier knots to use when attaching your leader, but I was a Tucker, and the nail knot was the only proper way to attach your line. My dad always tied it for me. I knew how, but my fingers lacked the coordination.

I tried over and over again. With each attempt, my hands started to shake a little more. Every failure made me more aware of my father's absence. I kept trying, but it was no use. The last attempt produced a tangled ball of line. I grabbed my fishing knife from my belt to cut it loose.

Then for the first time since my parents died, I cried. First a few drops, then a few more. My hands trembled as I cut the knot free with my knife...full streams were running down my cheeks. *Daddy...Daddy...I need you...* I kept repeating in my head. My hands were shaking, now totally incapable of tying anything.

I stopped trying to tie the knot. I let my tears continue to fall and I called for my dad a few more times in my head. Then I looked at my knife. It was time. Time to end the pain, time to take my life.

I put the blade to my wrist and prepared for what was to come. I braced myself for the pain. I counted down...3...2...

"Hey, what the hell are you doing, kid?" A stranger's voice stopped me right before I got to 1.

I turned around, startled, afraid of what the stranger may have seen. I watched the figure as he approached. My face wet with tears.

He was a young guy, probably just a few years older than me. He was wearing an old pair of Levis, a white t-shirt and an old wore down straw cowboy hat. As he got closer, he knelt down to look me right in the eye. His face was kind and I felt safe in his presence, but I also sensed his anger. The stranger was obviously mad.

"Give me that, you idiot!" He snatched the knife out of my hand and stood back up.

"C'mon...get up." He held out his hand.

I grabbed it and he pulled me back up to my feet.

I stood there waiting, not sure what to do...I knew I couldn't talk. He just looked me up a down and then huffed out a deep breath. The stranger then put his hand in his back pocket and pulled out a pouch of chewing tobacco...Red Man...I knew the brand...my grandpa gave it to me once...made me so sick I threw up...Mom said it served me right.

He placed a big wad of the stuff in his mouth and then allowed it to settle. He let a big stream of brown juice hit the ground before he started talking again. The noise of his saliva audible as it hit the earth.

"Now, I ain't sure exactly what you were planning, son, but it didn't look so good." He stopped and held out his hand.

"Name is Moose." He waited for me to shake his hand. I put out my hand, not sure what to do. He gripped it tightly as we shook hands; his grip was very strong.

"Don't worry...I know you can't talk." He winked.

My face must have looked lost, puzzled. Who was this guy? What kind of a name was Moose?...And how did he know about me?

"Your grandma's got a big mouth and Ennis is a small place. You ain't in Seattle anymore, kiddo. A fellow can't so much as take a crap in the woods around here without the whole town knowing about it." He stopped and gave me a serious look.

"Listen...I'll do you a favor...I won't tell your grandma about you and the knife...if you promise not to do it again...and if you let me fish with you. Or if you like, I just can just kick your ass for trying something so stupid." He stood and waited for my reply...I had no way to confirm the promise even though I agreed with the deal in my head.

"I'll take that as a yes," Moose smiled and patted my wet hair. He then spit a big wad of juice on the thirsty dirt.

Why was this guy being so nice? He must be the kind who is always trying to do right, the kind of guy who would take pity on a suicidal mute. Whatever the reason, I would take it. I wiped my

34

face clean with my shirt as the tears stopped. Moose just looked at me and smiled.

"You sure are a sight for sore eyes," he chuckled. "Okay, let's get your crap together and fish."

Moose walked over to my pole and grabbed my stuff without asking. I stood and watched, curious about this guy that just saved my life.

"I'm gonna throw a new leader on for you, David." Guess grandma also told Moose my name.

I waited patiently as Moose fixed my gear. He knew what he was doing and it only took a few minutes.

"There you go, good as new." Moose happily handed me my father's pole; the nail knot was flawless. I liked this guy.

"That's a nice rod you got there David…used to have one just like it myself." Moose kept talking as he got his own gear ready.

"Now how about we catch that fish you lost…whaddya say?"

I said nothing, but walked towards the Madison with my new friend. We fished the rest of the day. Moose was an excellent fisherman and we were a natural team. Without talking we were able to communicate and work the river together, just like my father and I used to. It was a day I never expected, a day that arrived not a moment too soon and without a second to spare.

The Madison valley was a picturesque sight: the beautiful, blue Montana sky, the eagles overhead, the sound of the breeze sprinting through the valley and the mountains hugging the horizon. In the middle of it all, here I was, fishing with a new friend. For the first time since the crash, I felt the pain of my life loosen its grip on my heart.

But friendship is precious; not only in the shade, but in the sunshine of life, and thanks to the benevolent arrangement the greater part of life is in the sunshine.
~Thomas Jefferson

Chapter Six

Grandma's smile was a mile wide when I returned. I smelled like fishing and my father's bag was full of the day's limit (I caught many more but only kept the best…the smaller fish would live to be caught another day). My grandma beamed as she observed the evidence of my success. Four beautiful rainbows and two brown trout slimed the inside of my father's bag. Without speaking my eyes told her about my day…and they spoke of more than darkness; there was a hint of happiness. I had Grandma, the Madison, and Moose to thank for that.

"Well, you must have worked up quite an appetite catching all those fish." My grandma spoke as I washed up. "Hamburgers sound okay?…Should be ready in just a few."

My grandma busily made her way around the kitchen setting the table. I finished washing up and tried to help. I noticed that I did have an appetite, I was really hungry, and I did look forward to eating. My stomach gurgled as the aroma flooded my nostrils.

Dinner was served and I took down a whole hamburger, a salad and I even had seconds of the macaroni salad. Grandma didn't say anything, she just gleefully observed. Her plan was working and she was proud. I was glad to see her enjoying the moment…I was enjoying it, too. I felt different and I knew that for the first time I was beginning to heal.

That evening Grandma and I sat in the living room, just like we did the night before. She reading as I listened to my music. I sat reflecting on the day as night settled in. I shivered whenever I thought about how close I came to taking my own life; I now felt foolish about it. If Moose hadn't have shown up it would all be over and I wouldn't be here with Grandma. I cringed at the thought, and then made myself a promise. I would try to live again; I would try to find my voice and my way out of the darkness. I had the momentum of today and I would use it.

I got up from the chair I was sitting on and I moved over to the couch near my grandma. There was room for two. My grandma looked up from her novel and lifted her eyes above her reading glasses. Her mouth lipped the words *love you*. My mind thought the same.

The next day I woke up excited. Again, a new emotion I hadn't experienced since the crash. Grandma didn't have to wake me up and I was up and in the shower much earlier than the day before. I put on a fresh change of clothes and met my grandma in the kitchen.

"Well, you are up early, Davey…you didn't give me much time to make breakfast…toast and juice will have to do." My grandma stood in the kitchen, still in her morning gown and slippers as she set my breakfast on the table.

"Lunch and gear are ready outside, I'm gonna get in the shower…just leave your stuff in the sink and I'll get it…have fun today, Davey." Grandma left me alone to finish my breakfast.

I ate it as fast as I could and I headed outside. It was still early enough that fresh dew covered everything in the shadows. Even in the summer months, Montana can be really cold in the morning, but the blue skies above meant it wouldn't be cold for long. Soon, the sun would take command and the cool waters of the Madison would be a welcome retreat. I grabbed dad's gear and my lunch and headed downstream, ready to catch more fish.

I wasn't too far from the drop-in spot when I spotted Moose. He was standing by the big rock, tying a new fly, getting ready to fish. I was happy to see him, I had hoped that he might want to fish with me again, but being a mute and all, I wondered if he grew bored of my company. I had never had an experience like this, where I immediately connected to a person and I was nervous it would end.

Luckily, Moose seemed happy to see me as well. He looked up from his line as I approached. Moose was wearing his old worn Cowboy hat, another white tee, and probably the same jeans as the day before. In his mouth another wad of chewing tobacco. This guy exuded Montana. He was rugged and peaceful, inviting but mysterious.

"Hey, David," Moose smiled. "Thought I might catch you here this morning. Beautiful ain't it?"

I just stared at Moose, not sure what to say even if I could talk.

"Montana, this river…it's amazing…sure would be a shame not to appreciate something as grand as what we have here…yep, every day is a gift, brother…I know you won't forget it." Moose tossed back my confiscated knife and I caught the blade.

He was right, I thought, *each day is a gift.*

Moose looked out at the water lost in thought, he took a deep breath. "Thanks for today Lord." Moose said out loud, but not towards me.

I sat my gear down and began preparing for the day. I had a lot of luck with nymph flies yesterday so I selected a dark black one from my dad's fly selection, which he had kept safely stored in a small box in the upper right pocket of his fishing jacket, just like me. I noticed some waders lying by Moose's stuff.

"Brought you a pair." Moose noticed my wandering eyes. "Figured we could really fish the Madison today…I don't wanna pass up any stretch on account of not being prepared."

Again, I really liked this guy. Waders would allow us to get waist deep in the river with no problems, something that held us back yesterday. I had a pair, but like grandma said, she couldn't find my stuff and I was glad that she hadn't. I liked using my dad's gear, it made it like he was still kind of with me,

40

and now with the addition of waders it was perfect. It was like Moose could read my mind.

I finished getting set up and I slid into the waders that Moose brought for me. We were all set and ready to go. We stood by the water for a brief moment, surveying the current. This moment, the moment before the first cast brought back vivid memories of fishing with my father. But today those memories seemed less sad, instead of sorrow I felt lucky to have them. I felt lucky that this river ran through me and my family. I felt my father with me.

"Let's catch some fish, Champ." Moose slapped me on the back as he moved past and towards the river.

I doubt Moose knew the significance of the word *Champ*, but I sure did. I knew then and there that somehow, somewhere my father was with me. Not just a superstitious hope. Not just a cliché of heaven. Goose bumps stood on my arm, I felt my eyes water just a bit. Moose was already in the water, his fly traveling gracefully through the air.

"Let's go!" Moose yelled towards me. "We got a lot of river to cover and I ain't waiting."

I stepped into the water just as a fish jumped about twenty yards south of my position. *Ok, Dad,* I thought. *Let's catch some fish.*

When we understand the outside of things we think we have them. Yet the Lord puts his things in sub defined, suggestive shapes, yielding no satisfactory meaning to the mere intellect, but unfolding themselves to the conscious and heart.
~George MacDonald

Chapter Seven

The days began blending together, each day just as great as the one before. Most days, Moose fished with me. Some days he had to hang out with "his girl" or visit his "pop"; those days, I fished alone. Grandma was having a blast cooking the fresh river trout that I brought home. Trout and scrambled eggs was becoming my favorite breakfast meal. Our nighttime routine had become tradition (reading and music, followed by my early departure to bed). Each morning was breakfast and then out the door.

It was obvious I was getting better. Suicide was a distant memory. My appetite was normal. My face looked healthier in the mirror and I had actually even smiled a time or two…Moose made a big deal out of it when he saw one. But I was obviously still sick…I still couldn't talk. I couldn't understand why…it was just a ledge that felt too scary to jump off of. I could tell that Moose and Grandma were waiting for my voice but they never pushed…I was very glad for that…I was lucky to have them.

Another morning was underway and another full day of fishing ahead. I tried to calculate out how long I had been in Ennis…I figured about a month. Yesterday I fished alone so I was hoping to see Moose as I walked to our usual spot. He had said that he would be available today.

Sure enough, he was there. But he didn't look like a fisherman. As I approached it was obvious that Moose had no plans of fishing. His hair was freshly combed, no cowboy hat. He was wearing a newer pair of jeans and a nice flannel shirt. He

44

had a fresh shave, which looked funny to me as I had only seen Moose with a scruffy one-day shadow. He smiled and walked to meet me as I approached.

"David, how's it going, brother?" Moose always liked to ask me questions even though he knew I wasn't going to answer. He slapped me on the shoulder and continued. "Listen, can't fish today…gotta hang out with the woman…thought I'd let you know…I know I said I could fish today but sometimes you gotta listen to your lady…sorry, Davey."

My heart dropped a little but I tried not to let it show. Moose was spending a ton of time with me and it was understandable that he just couldn't fish every day. Moose looked at me, probably detecting my disappointment.

"Listen." Moose's eyes lit up. "My girl's been dying to meet you. I know she wouldn't mind if you tagged along." Moose paused. "What do you say?"

I nodded.

"Holy crap, kid!" I think you just said yes. "You're gonna be talking in no time, yep, I'll be damned." Moose was proud of my small accomplishment. "Alright, then…truck is by the road. You can throw your gear in the back. Let's go."

I walked up to the truck with Moose. It was an old baby blue Ford F-150 with two doors. I hopped in and sat on the passenger side of the big truck. Moose fired up the engine and we headed out.

Curiosity came to mind. I had never seen Moose's truck; new questions formed. Where did he live? Where did his girlfriend live? I knew he had a "pop" which he talked about every now and then. I really wanted to ask questions and I realized I knew little about my friend and his life.

Moose turned the wheel and we left. Soon we were driving through downtown Ennis. We passed the top of the hill where a statue of an old fisherman stood as a reminder of what Ennis was all about. We passed its cafés, fishing shops, motels and bars. As we exited town the road bridged back over the

Madison; a few fisherman were out on the water and several drift boats were getting ready by the launch.

Moose then made a left as we left Ennis which put us on Jeffers road. Jeffers was technically its own town but any outsider would consider it a part of Ennis. I knew it well.

Moose stepped on the gas as we bumped our way down the long straight dirt road, surrounded by miles of open prairie. A large dust cloud trailed behind, produced as the dry earth met the wheels of Moose's F-150. Moose seemed lost in thought and so was I.

Jeffers was where we used to go to church when I was little. After a few minutes, I could see the little church up ahead and Jeffers (which was really just a collection of a few farm houses). Jeffers was special. Besides being home to our family church, it was also the gateway to one of my favorite camping destinations, Jack Creek. Jack Creek is a small tributary stream that feeds the Madison and its history fills my mind with s'mores, campfires, tents, wildlife and hiking. My grandpa used to live on Jack Creek when he was a young man, breaking horses for a living, a real cowboy. I couldn't believe Moose had roots in these parts as well, but then again Moose seemed like family.

The small church in the distance became larger and I realized it was our destination. It wasn't Sunday so I was a little confused when Moose's truck slowed to a stop right by the old, one story building.

"So, gotta be honest with you kid," Moose began to talk but he didn't turn the engine off. "This is kind of a set-up."

I was lost and gave a puzzled look back. What the hell was going on?

"See, my lady, she's the kind of gal that is a natural healer…I figured I could only help you so much…she really wants to meet you…I think if you spent some time alone with her, she could help…so that's the plan…okay."

Why did Moose trick me? I didn't want to spend a good fishing day stuck in a church with a stranger. And why all of a sudden did Moose want to "fix" me? He never hassled me before. This didn't feel right. I shook my head…I shook it again and crossed my arms, using my newly acquired communication skills. I wasn't the kind to be set-up like this.

"You ain't got a choice…" Moose responded to my reaction.

We both sat in silence for a few minutes; I wasn't sure what to do. I was miles away from Grandma's…way too far to walk…but the last thing I needed was another therapy session…unpleasant memories of Bellingham came to mind.

"Hey, I saved your life right…just do me this favor…you owe me one."

Moose was right. I did owe him one. As much as I didn't like it, I opened the truck door. I didn't want to disappoint my friend, even if he was dishonest about his intentions today. I stepped out and closed the door. Moose didn't get out. He rolled down the window.

"Listen, I'm going up to Jack Creek to see Pop today. I have been spending so much time fishing with you and hanging out with my girl lately…this will be a perfect opportunity to visit the old man."

I made eye contact to confirm. I couldn't be mad at Moose…he was just too nice, and the thought of him spending time with his dad made sense. If my dad was up at Jack Creek I would be sprinting up there to see him. Moose's dad was still alive and that was a good thing, something to appreciate.

"Later, David, I'll be back at four and I'll get you back to your grandma's by supper," Moose shouted as he drove away.

I looked at my watch. It was only ten o'clock in the morning. What the heck was I going to do with a complete stranger for six hours? I stood outside staring at the entrance to the little building, not ready to go inside.

Just as a candle cannot burn without fire, men cannot live without a spiritual life.
~Buddha

Chapter Eight

The church looked so quiet and lonely. It was a peaceful sight, all alone in the middle of the Madison Valley. Its only company was a couple of old maple trees, which provided much-welcomed shade during the summer, and the sprinkling of a few homes here and there. As the quiet breeze whistled through the countryside, I still hadn't moved, not ready to go inside. My muscles were tight and my breathing was heavy. Moose was long gone by now. A dissipating cloud of dust was the only reminder of his presence. *Who was Moose's girlfriend and why did I have to spend the day with her? He obviously trusted her so maybe I could?*

Then I heard a beautiful noise. Immediately my tension began to lift. Inside the steeple echoed an angelic sound. A women's voice began singing "Agnus Dei." The sound was so perfect it seemed like it was pouring from heaven, my breathing slowed down and my muscles relaxed. I realized why I was having such a positive reaction to the music; it was my mother's favorite song. She used to hum and sing it all the time. I closed my eyes and I let the music grab my soul. I began walking towards the door. Her words bounced against the walls and into my chest. Warm memories of church, God and my mother surrounded me. The words went…

Halleleluah, Halleleluuahah, Holy, Holy
Are you Lord God Almighty
Worthy is the Lamb, Worthy is the Lamb
You are holy…holy

50

For the Lord God Almighty reigns…

The entrance door to the church was already half open so I slid right into the building without making a noise. The church was empty and the women's voice echoed against the walls. I walked past the vacant rows and towards the front. She had her back to me and was kneeling at the altar. I quietly approached but I didn't want to disturb. I sat in the front pew and let her finish the song. When it was over she stood up and said, "Thank you, Lord," then turned to face me.

She was as beautiful as her voice. Her straight brown hair ran to her shoulders and her warm brown eyes welcomed me. She looked about the same age as Moose and I immediately could envision the pair. *A good couple,* I thought. She was wearing an all-white summer dress and a bracelet made of flowers, her brown hair seemed weightless. But above all, it was her smile that was the most peaceful thing about her.

"Hello, Davey." She spoke as if she already knew me. "I have been waiting a long time to see you."

Waiting a long time? That didn't make any sense.

"I thought we could have a picnic today in the fields. It's such a lovely day. Does that sound alright?" she asked.

I nodded and she smiled.

"Wonderful!" she exclaimed and then bent over to grab a basket. "Would you mind carrying this, it's our food for later." She handed me a large wicker basket covered with a checkered cloth. I grabbed the container which felt surprisingly light.

"Alright…let's go for a walk." The young lady headed out of the church and I followed.

Leaving the church, we headed out on a small dirt trail which ran parallel to the road. At that moment the breeze picked up which caused the cloth in the basket to blow open. I quickly grabbed the cloth and immediately tried to cover the food when I noticed the strangest thing. The basket was completely empty…no wonder it felt so light. *This girl must be nuts…*but she seemed so perfect and nice. The trail split off from the road and

51

into a large field, nothing around us but long wild grass rustling in the breeze. Off in the distance I spotted a large isolated oak tree. My companion didn't say anything; she just hummed hymns the whole way.

As we approached the tree I noticed the Montana sun had warmed the landscape and my body. The shade of the big oak was a welcome relief. Already waiting for us, in the shade, was a blanket. It was spread out and held down by rocks on its corners...*just like how we used to picnic.*

"Sit down, Davey," the girl motioned. "Blessed are those who mourn, for they will find comfort."

Okay, this lady, as nice as she was, was getting a little weird. I sat down, not sure of what to do next. I knew we had no food, so no need digging into the basket.

"David, can I tell you a story?" She sat down next to me, her eyes making contact with mine. She placed her hand on my knee. I nodded.

"A long time ago, when I was a little girl, I experienced tragedy. I felt pain much like what you are feeling. I know pain, Davey, just like you...and I have experienced love...a love greater than the pain. See my story starts with my father...I didn't have a great father like yours..."

She paused, probably because of my grimace and confused expression. How could she know my pain and how the hell does she know anything about my dad?

"Your dad is thoughtful and kind," she continued. "Mine was a drunk, and many nights we would suffer the abuse of his drunk hand...it was just me and my mom...my mom protected and loved me...she made a plan for us to escape the torture, but when my father found out he beat her so bad, Davey..." She paused...and then slowly spoke "He beat her to death."

She stopped to look me in the eye. I wouldn't have ever been able to guess that someone so lovely could have ever experienced such a horrible thing. She looked at the sky, closed her eyes and took a deep breath. Then she continued.

"My dad spent the rest his life in prison. My journey was quite painful, at times I almost took my life...I drank for many years...but your father, he rescued me...and our Father, God, he always rescues and protects us...sometimes His greatest protection comes at times when He feels furthest away...I understand that now and someday you will as well."

My eyes must have lit up...how in the world was my father connected to her story? She couldn't have been more than seventeen; we moved away from Ennis long before these events could have happened.

"I know you have questions, kiddo, one day it will make sense...but this is what I want you to understand. Even through the greatest of pain, life is still good. Even through the greatest of loss, you can find everything. Your Father in heaven loves you so much, and your earthly dad does as well. They are still with you son and they will never leave. Neither will your mom..."

She stopped and I noticed the tear tracks forming on her face. I looked down at the blanket and watched as drops from my own eyes fell to the blanket. My vision blurred as I cried faster and harder than I have ever experienced. My body began to shake uncontrollably. She threw hers arms around me and held me tight; I felt her tears falling on my shoulder. Then I burst.

"But, they are not coming back!" I shouted. "T-t-t-they're, g-g-gone. Gone!" I stuttered, trembling as my body released the pressure. "My sister that I never met, my dad, my mom," I cried. "It hurts so bad!"

"Not everything is as it seems; life is much bigger than death." She moved back to look me in the eye. She began wiping my face with her hand as I hyperventilated. "It's ok Sweetheart. It's ok," she kept repeating. "It's ok. It's ok...breath."

When I calmed down we looked at each other and paused. A big smile swept across my new friend's face.

"Guess what you just did, David?"

"I spoke," I answered back, surprised.

It was weird to hear my own voice, something I hadn't heard in almost ten months. Sometimes, I had wondered if I could still do it. It felt like the greatest accomplishment of my life.

"That's right, kiddo, you spoke," and then we both broke into joyous laughter. I had never felt so close to a person in such a little amount of time, not even Moose. Moose saved my life and now his girlfriend gave me life.

"You hungry?" she asked.

"We have no food, ma'am," I answered.

"Like I said Davey, things aren't always as they seem." She moved the basket closer to us. "Take a look."

I pulled back the checkered cloth. Inside lay two Cokes, two apples, and two delicious looking sandwiches. I froze in shock.

"How...did...what...the?" I asked.

"Blessed are those who mourn, for they will find comfort, David." She said, "What was lost and gone will be found, what is empty will be full."

This was the second time she had said those words, but this time I made the connection. She was quoting a Bible story...or parts of one anyway, some sermon that Jesus gave about comfort and protection. I never cared too much for the Bible, its words distant and often times irrelevant, but here at this moment those words felt true for the first time. I now could safely mourn the loss of my parents. I had the comfort of Moose, Moose's Girlfriend, Grandma and I guess God...whoever or whatever He was. I cried a little more.

After lunch we walked the fields and continued to talk. I told her all about Bellingham and how my parents died. We both laughed and told stories about Moose. She told me about her mom and that how after her death she could still feel her comfort. Every time the breeze picked up I could feel the presence of God. This was the greatest afternoon of my life.

We strolled back to the church right around three-thirty. Moose was already there standing by his truck, patiently waiting for our return.

"Hey, good-looking," he yelled toward my new friend as we approached. "I haven't been replaced now have I?" he chuckled.

"Baby, no one can replace you," she called back.

When we got to the truck they embraced for a big hug and kiss. I turned away so they could have their privacy. Moose then escorted her into the church and I waited outside for ten minutes or so. I stood by the Ford patiently, ready to tell him the good news.

Perhaps they are not stars, but rather openings in heaven, where the love of our lost ones pours through and shines down upon us to let us know that they are happy.
~*Eskimo Proverb*

Chapter Nine

"She's something else, huh?" Moose asked as his truck bumped its way down Jeffers Road and back towards Ennis.

"Yeah, she's amazing," I answered.

"You bet she is. I spend weeks fishing with you...not a peep, and just a few hours with her...she's a miracle worker that one," he smiled, a man deeply in love.

"She is...and literally, I mean she made food appear out of nowhere," I answered back.

"Ha! That old trick...my pop used that once on me...na, I don't think she can take full credit for that one kid," Moose laughed. "But a little meal is nothing compared to the real miracle, you're back buddy...you're talking!"

Who are these people? Maybe they were angels? They sure acted the part...and apparently miracles are no big deal to them, which seems about right for an angel. All I knew is that they were my friends and they weren't ordinary. I quietly thanked God for placing them in my life.

"Hey, Moose," I asked.

"Yeah," Moose answered as we turned off of Jeffers and into downtown Ennis.

"Thanks." Words couldn't describe my gratitude.

"No need to thank me, buddy." He turned to give me a wink.

"No, really...thanks," I repeated.

"I know, Champ," he said it again. The word *champ*…so significant I wondered if he knew. I wasn't sure, but it sure seemed like it.

"My dad used to call me that, Moose." Then, I asked, "Did you already know that?" I had the feeling he did.

"Sure," he simply answered.

"But how?" I questioned.

"Because that seems like an appropriate name for a kid like you." Moose changed the subject. "Listen, I am gonna be heading out of town tomorrow night, but I was hoping we could fish the morning together…You want to hit the river extra early with me?"

"Absolutely," I answered.

"Okay, extra early…meet you by the rock at sunrise." Moose grinned.

"Sure sunrise," I confirmed.

"And I thought later on you could meet my friend…if you don't mind?" Moose asked.

"Nah, I don't mind." Any friend of Moose's was a friend of mine. "Hey," I wondered, "does your friend have any special gifts…you know like your girlfriend…?"

Moose just burst into laughter, slapping the steering wheel as we pulled up to Grandma's house.

"What's so funny?" I wondered.

"Yeah, kid, my buddy has a few special gifts," Moose answered.

I got out of the truck and grabbed my gear as the motor of Moose's truck idled, not sure why my question seemed so funny. Moose threw it in reverse and gave a whistle.

"See you tomorrow buddy, remember…sunrise," he yelled as he pulled away.

I walked around to the back porch and placed my fishing gear in the corner. It was empty, but I had a feeling Grandma wouldn't mind. I opened the back slider and let myself inside. Grandma was in the kitchen with her back turned preparing supper. I walked up to her and placed my hand on her shoulder.

"Hey, Grandma," I said, excited and proud to have my voice back.

"Ohh!" she jumped in shock. "You startled me Davey; you can't be sneaking up on an old lady like that." Then she paused and gave me a stunned look, "Wait—what did you just say? You spoke, right?"

"I said 'hey Grandma'," I said, nice and slow with a big smile.

She threw her arms around me and laughed a big joyous laugh.

"I knew it, Davey; I knew it. I knew it...I'll be damned! My grandson is back."

"Yeah, I think I am," I smiled.

"You betcha you are!" She was so happy. "When did it start? Just now?" she asked.

"Earlier today when I was with a friend," I answered.

"Friend? Okay we have a lot of catching up to do. What friend?" she asked.

"Moose...well not actually Moose, his girlfriend heard me first then him," I tried to explain.

"Moose...huh...," something I said caused Grandma to pause, her face looked caught in thought.

"I think you know him Grandma...he knows you, said you told him about me and how I couldn't talk. And he has been like my best friend lately...when I go out fishing he usually joins me...and today he took me to the old church in Jeffers. That's where I met his girlfriend and got healed." I had so much to tell her.

"So...I wasn't dreaming," Grandma replied, but more to herself then to me.

"Huh...do you know him, Grandma?" I tried to center the conversation. "I think they attend the old church in Jeffers...that's where Moose took me today."

My Grandma's skin lost its color and her eyes got real wide. "Davey, I need to sit down." She made her way to the living room to sit down in her favorite chair.

"Grandma, what's going on?" I asked.

"Just give me a second to think, okay Davey?" She paused, "Can you grab me a drink from the kitchen."

"Sure, what do you want?"

"Scotch!" she said immediately. "Grab the bottle of Johnny Walker. It's above the fridge…and better grab two glasses…I think this is a scotch conversation for the both of us."

Scotch? I wondered. *Grandma rarely drinks and I have only had a few sips of beer in my life. This was big, real big.*

I grabbed the bottle and two glasses from the kitchen and made my way back into the living room. My grandma took the bottle and then one of the glasses. She gave both our cups a generous pour. I sat down, wondering what to say or what she would say.

"Davey, you said that you went to the old Jeffers Church today. Did I hear you right?" Grandma asked.

"Yeah, the one we all use to go to when I was little." I was thrown off by the question.

"David," she paused and took a sip from the scotch, her eyes were looking out past me and out the window. "David…that church burned down last summer."

No way, I thought, *couldn't be… I was just there.*

"Maybe they rebuilt it, Grandma?" I responded with logic.

"You're right they did," she answered. "But they rebuilt it on the other side of Ennis…there isn't a church in Jeffers anymore…they sold the land…it's a dude ranch now."

My heart skipped a beat and I felt lightheaded. I tried to take a few deep breaths as I processed the information. *Oh crap,* I thought. *What if I wasn't better? What if I was full-fledged crazy?*

"Take a sip of your drink, David, just relax," she calmly kept talking. "Don't worry. I think I have an explanation." She got up from her chair and walked over to the coffee table. Under the table was a large photo album. It had always been there but I never paid any attention to it. I took a gulp of the scotch. It was horrible…the strong liquid burned my throat and my chest. I let out a loud cough.

"Easy, Davey," she said. "That stuff is made for sipping." She placed the album in my lap and she sat back down. I sat my drink down on the nightstand next to my chair. I didn't mind parting with the stuff; it was way too strong for me. I placed my hand on the album and went to open the cover.

"Wait, Davey. Before you open that let me tell you a story." She stopped my action.

"Okay," I said.

"Your daddy was a strong boy, just like your grandpa. He was strong in all sorts of ways; he was physically strong but more importantly…he was morally strong. He was always looking out for others, helping a neighbor build a fence, sticking up for a kid that others were making fun of…your dad just had this special strong heart. I knew it made perfect sense when he fell in love with your mother. Your mother moved to Ennis with all sorts of pain from her childhood…your father, he loved her back to health…and that girl loved him so much for it"

"Wait," I interrupted, "my mom had a tough childhood?" I asked. I never knew much about my mother's upbringing. She just always said that her parents died before I was born and that they were never really that close.

"Oh, yes," my grandma answered. "Bless her heart, that girl had a tough go. But she was strong just like your daddy. But, like I said, your daddy embodied strength, everyone could just sense that about him…which is why everyone in Ennis called him by his nickname. No, people didn't call him James Tucker around here."

"What did they call him?" I asked.

"Why don't you open the album now," she whispered…

I opened the thick cover and began turning the pages. The first few pages were some really old photos. My grandma sat quietly, patiently observing as I flipped through the album.

"That's your grandpa and me when we were young." She leaned in so she could get a better look at the pictures. "Keep going, Davey." She seemed really excited.

I turned a few more pages and got to some photos that obviously were of my dad and my aunt when they were babies. I turned again and found some more photos containing my grandpa, grandma and my aunt and dad as young kids. Then I turned the next page and felt a frozen chill. Goosebumps covered every hair follicle on my body; my neck tightened and my heart skipped frantically.

There on the next page was a young man, probably in his late teens. He was standing by the rock where I almost committed suicide. He was wearing jeans, a white t-shirt and an old cowboy hat. He was my best friend. I looked up at my grandma.

"Did they call my daddy "Moose", Grandma?" I already knew the answer.

"Yes, David, they called him Moose." My grandma had tears in her eyes.

"What's happening, Grandma?" my tears joined hers.

"I'm not sure, Davey." She moved over to throw her arms around me, "I guess the grave can't hold back love, kiddo."

"Is this real?" I asked.

"As real as that river out there," she replied.

"Am I crazy?"

"No, Davey, no you are not crazy."

"What do we do now? I'm confused, Grandma." My mind tried to understand this new reality.

"I don't know dear. I am as confused as you...but I believe it will all make sense soon," she responded. "Now tell me about your daddy and where you have been...I want to hear everything," she beamed a joyous face like I have never seen before as I began tell her about my adventures.

We talked for hours that night. We finished the scotch (mostly due to my grandma), and we had a late dinner. My grandma took me through the whole photo album and I heard stories about my family that I never even knew. We offered our best guesses as to what was happening, but we knew that whatever it was, it wasn't our imagination. We talked about God and the afterlife…we were in shock but we weren't scared. The only thing we knew for sure was that our family was full of love and that something else, something more than just this life was in store. It was late when we turned in for bed but our final conversation was the most interesting of all.

"Grandma," I said as I got into bed and she followed to turn off the lights.

"Yes, David," she answered.

"I am gonna get up real early tomorrow. Moose said he has a big day planned for me," I told her.

"I know," she replied.

"How do you know?" I wondered.

"Your grandpa's been visiting me in my dreams…he told me about it." She smiled.

"How come you waited until now to tell me?" I asked.

"Because," she paused, "we've been talking about stuff that might scare you…about my health and such…I didn't want to give you more than you could handle."

"Should I be scared, Grandma?" I asked.

"Heaven's no, Davey. Heaven's no."

Miracles are not contrary to nature, but only contrary to what we know about nature.
~Saint Augustine

Chapter Ten

I set my alarm for five o'clock, even though I didn't need an alarm. I barely slept a wink as the many thoughts ran through my mind. I was talking. Moose was my dad and his girlfriend my mom; tomorrow I would see them again. I rested a little out of pure exhaustion, but when the alarm sounded I sprang into action, ready to face the most exciting day of my life.

I took a short shower and had a quick bowl of cereal. My grandma was still in bed and I could hear her snores as I quietly walked outside and into the early dawn. I grabbed my fishing gear and headed downstream, moving quickly with anticipation.

When I approached the rock the sun was just starting to appear on the horizon. Moose was visible but he was right in the sun's glare. I was jogging by this time but once I saw him I sprinted.

"Dad!..Dad!" I yelled as I approached the figure. Then I noticed he was running to me as well.

We collided like two football players. A big hug ensued and then Moose threw me up in the air laughing.

"So, I guess my cover is blown, huh," he chuckled.

I felt dumb, looking at his face now; I wondered how I missed it. This was obviously my dad, just a little younger and a little happier.

"How come you didn't tell me?" I asked.

"Would that have mattered?" he said.

"Yeah, you bet it would!" I replied.

"Not everything in life is fact, Son. Life isn't all about what we know, not everything is questions and answers. Sometimes we miss everything because we are so concerned with details, so concerned with knowing," he answered in riddle.

"Huh?" I was dumbfounded.

"Yeah, "huh" is right," he smiled. "Listen we only have the morning before we got to go...you want to fish this stretch one last time buddy...me and you."

"*One last time,*" I wondered, "what does that mean, Dad...*is* this the last time?"

"Like I said, just live, Son, don't worry...you'll miss it," he cut me off.

"But why do we have to leave?" Panic was in my voice.

My dad walked over to me and placed his hand on my shoulder.

"Don't worry, Son," he spoke, "just listen."

"To what?" I asked.

"Close your eyes." He directed and I obeyed. "Now just listen...listen to the water, listen to the wind, listen to creation."

My eyes remained closed and my father's hand rested on my shoulder. At first I just heard my thoughts, but my father's hand and his presence kept calming me. My mind wanted to ask questions; it wanted to worry.

"Shhh." My father's voice pushed the anxiety away. I once again tried to listen.

My ears opened up. I heard the Madison's running water; I felt the sun warming the landscape. The noise of life was around me. Insects were buzzing and birds were singing in the trees. The breeze kissed my skin. Then I heard God. I heard love and nothing else. I opened my eyes and looked at Moose.

"No fear, Son, only love." He beamed with happiness.

He was right, a giant weight lifted off of my shoulders and the worries floated away. We stood for a few moments just looking at one another.

"I'm ready to fish with you, Dad," I said.

"Me too, Son, me too," he replied.

We hit the river and fished away. Throughout the morning I kept realizing how special this moment was and I knew that this time would be with me forever; this feeling and this connection I had with my dad would never pass. Fears of death and loss no longer had a grip on my heart. I was free. I was fishing with my dad.

My fly traveled through the air as my instincts brought me to a nice ripple in the river. It landed softly and I watched as it drifted a few feet and then I felt it. At this point in the summer I had caught dozens of fish, but this one...instantly I knew...I knew it was a special fish.

The fish hit the fly hard and immediately she ran. Without any effort she was stripping out my line. I tried to keep the line tight as the energy of this particular fish was like nothing I had ever felt. The sound of my reel surrendering its line to the fish caught my dad's attention. He reeled in and I heard him sloshing his way in the river towards me.

"Looks like you got a battle on your hands," he yelled over the current as he made his way to my location. Just then, the fish jumped. The sight of her was amazing. She was the biggest trout I had ever seen. Her rainbow skin caught the sun as she flew through the air. She was so massive that when she landed back in the river she made a splash just like a large rock. My pole was bent so tight it almost made a perfect "u" shape.

"WHOO...YEAAH...Don't let her go, Son!!" my dad yelled. I could tell he was just as excited and just as nervous as I was. I dared not reel for fear that I would break the line. My only chance to bring her in would be when she tired. I only had six pound test line on...barely enough to hold the fish's force, let alone the tension reeling would cause. I watched the water and my reel...I was running out of line. By this time my father was standing right next to me, as excited and drawn in as if he was watching the final play of the Super Bowl.

We were standing in a deeper section of the river and the water was running up and around my lower back as I tried to hold my ground. The river was very fast in this section, terrible

70

conditions for pulling in a monster like this. I looked down at my reel as my line was getting down to its backing...I didn't have much time and if this fish didn't tire soon I was going to lose her. Downstream was a slower section of river, shallow water and a beach. This is where I needed to be...and if I wanted to pull in this beast it was where I had to be.

My plan was set. I looked at my dad and gave him a smile.

"Go get'em, Champ!" he yelled.

I lifted my feet and released myself to the power of the river. Water completely engulfed me and I floated with the current, as my whole physical being felt as one with the river. A memory came back to me as my head submerged under the water...I remembered my baptism so many years earlier. I remember the feeling of God connecting with me in the water. I continued to drift with the white water...soon the river slowed down and I swam towards the beach, keeping a firm hold on my fishing pole. As I stood back up in the shallow section, I felt as if I was that young child again, helpless and surrounded by something good and something greater than myself.

My plan had worked and, from my new location, I was able to reel. At this point the fish was exhausted from her battle and I was able to pull her in safely. My hair and clothes were completely drenched, evidence of a risk well worth the reward. In the distance I could hear my father approaching through the brush as I brought in the fish.

She was massive, a full grown rainbow with beautiful scales of all colors running down her side. Her weight was heavy as I held her in my hands. As she breathed I noticed the orange stripes under her jaw, she was a rare cutthroat rainbow trout, a true blue-ribbon prize fish. I measured her length against my fishing bag, twenty-four inches! This was the biggest catch of my life. As blood ran out of her gills I checked the line and noticed that she swallowed my fly, probably the reason I didn't lose her when I drifted in the water. It was then that I realized that the person approaching wasn't my father but another man.

Just like when I first met Moose, this man and his presence felt right and he had a calming effect on me. He was shorter than my dad, probably around 5'10. He had dark skin and his long black hair was pulled into a pony tail. He wore brown sandals, some brown cargo shorts and a white v-neck tee shirt. He had a well groomed short black beard with a few moles and freckles splashed across his face. His eyes were warm, inviting and very peaceful. He was only a few steps away and he smiled, observing my catch.

"Quite an impressive fish," he spoke as he walked towards me.

"Thanks," I said proudly. "It's the biggest one of my life...did you happen to see my dad? I want to show him." I asked.

"Your dad is with your family, but trust me he saw you catch this fish," the man smiled. His teeth were a little crooked but something about him just seemed so beautiful.

I looked down at my fish. She was lying on the bank and her blood and slime were beginning to coat the sand she was twitching in.

"What are you going to do with her?" the man asked.

"I don't know," I replied, "probably go to a taxidermist and have it mounted."

"She is beautiful," he said. "How about you let her run free again in the river?"

"She's gonna die, sir, she swallowed the hook," I answered.

"Oh, I'm not so sure about that, Son," he replied.

"No, really...look," I held the fish up by the line; her body was barely moving and bleeding heavily. "She's all but dead now."

"What if I could make her better? Would you agree to her freedom?" he asked. I could feel his tenderness and compassion. I found it weird that he was asking my permission. If he was capable of such a thing I obviously couldn't stand in his way.

"Sure," I replied. I was willing to part with my trophy if he was able to hold up to his end of the deal.

"Thank you," he said softly. Then he crouched down and placed his hands on the dying fish. His hands were large and I couldn't see exactly what he was doing even though my eyes were glued. He gave a quick tug on the line and handed me my fly. Then, holding the lifeless fish in his hands he turned towards the river.

Next to our location, the water was very shallow, only a few inches deep and barely any current. He placed the massive cutthroat in the water, her blood running through the cracks of his fingers and covering his hands. Then he just remained still for a moment. His eyes were closed and he was bent over, holding a dead fish in the water.

"My love makes all things new," he said and released the fish. I crept closer and stood right over the trout...watching. At first she was lifeless, then she moved...first just a quick twitch, and then she bolted out of the shallow section, through some half submerged rocks and back to her home, kicking up water as she splashed away. He watched too and laughed with satisfaction.

I was amazed, but after all I had learned in the past day I wasn't shocked. It was impossible and it happened. This fit my new framework and understanding of life.

The man washed his bloody hands in the stream and then stood back up.

"Are you my dad's friend?" I asked the man. He was smiling, staring out at the path the fish took to find freedom. He turned to me to answer the question.

"Yes...and I am your friend too, Son," he said as a big smile swept across his face. The kind of smile that suggested he knew something that I didn't, but that he couldn't wait to share.

This man was obviously special. I wondered if he was dead like my parents and I wondered how he and my dad became friends. He said we were friends too. Even though we just met, I agreed.

"Who are you?" I asked.

"Come with me and I will show you." He motioned to the trailhead from which he had come.

So I say to you: Ask and it will be given to you; seek and you will find; knock and the door will be opened to you.
~Luke 11:9

Chapter Eleven

My curiosity about this man was piqued. I followed as
we made our way through the brush and into a heavily forested
trail. I knew this area well, so I was surprised by the surroundin-
gs; there were no dense forests in the valley…something
mysterious was happening.

"Sir, where are we?" I asked as I walked briskly trying to
keep up with his graceful strides.

"Look around, David, doesn't this look familiar?" he
answered back.

My eyes scanned the wilderness and I spotted a stream
off in the distance. Memories quickly came back and I was able
to identify the location.

"Jack Creek!" I yelled.

We were in the mountains next to Ennis. Obviously this
was another miracle and perhaps the coolest yet; we had covered
several miles in only a few minutes of walking. The smell of the
fresh pine trees entered my nostrils and all the nostalgia of this
location came back. Memories of campfires, fishing with worms,
picnics, family, and most of all memories of love.

"This is the special place I have set aside for your
family," the man said as we approached the end of the trail and
he pointed to a clearing in the trees. We walked out into the
clearing and stood above a meadow. I remembered hiking to
this location once many years ago. It was far from our normal
campsite but it was beautiful and well worth the trek.

Down below in the meadow I saw my dad and my mom, but this time in their older bodies, just as I remembered them, before the crash. They were far away but I knew it was them. They had a blanket laid out as they sat under the sun, holding each other. They looked so peaceful and perfect. I just contently watched, not wanting to disturb the scene.

"Wonderful isn't it?" The man spoke. "Love…what a joy it is to my heart."

He was right. My heart felt so full watching my parents bask in the sun, everything seemed right. I was so full of joy that my eyes were beginning to well up with moisture. My trance of happiness was broken by a tug on my shorts.

I looked down and saw a little girl standing next to me. Her hair was blonde and in pigtails. She was wearing a yellow summer dress woven together with white lace. Her feet were bare and covered with mountain dust and grass stains.

"Can I have a hug?" she asked.

"Sure," I replied. She was so cute…how could I say no?

Immediately she threw her arms around me and I picked her up from the ground. My heart pounded and I felt the warm feeling of love covering my entire body. There was a connection between this little girl and me, and I immediately was able to identify what it was. She was family.

"Hi, I'm your sister. Someday we will get to play together all the time here." Her grip tightened around my neck and I hugged her back as tightly as I could. I knew who she was and I immediately broke into tears upon confirmation.

"I dreamt of you," I sobbed.

"I know, big brother," she replied. "Sometimes I dream about you, too…don't be sad." She gave a big, innocent kiss on my cheek smearing my tears. "Brian says I just have to be patient…that you will be here soon."

"Who's Brian?" I asked.

"My buddy," she said. "He is really sorry, don't be mad at him, okay…he's my best friend."

"Ok," I didn't understand but I kept hugging my little sister.

My eyes caught the man who brought me here. He was crying a little too.

"Ok sweetheart, your brother and I have to go," he said.

She immediately released her grip and her little feet hit the ground.

"No, we aren't going anywhere!" I yelled. I was going down to the meadow to be with my family.

My sister looked up at me with a confused look. Then she giggled, like I just told a funny joke.

"He always takes care of you, big brother…trust him." She pointed to the man.

My emotions wanted to resist but the purity of my sister, the purity of this man and his nature told me to obey.

"Okay," I said reluctantly, wiping the tears from my face.

"See you later, alligator." She smiled and then began sprinting down the hill towards my parents in the meadow. I watched her little legs motor her towards the picnic and then she jumped on my parents as all three wrestled in the field. I wanted so bad to follow, to be with them…that was my family…I needed them so much. The man placed his hand on my shoulder for comfort. I turned to look back and he was staring at me.

"You are so special to me," he said.

At this point I was pretty sure I knew who he was. I wanted to ask but I was afraid…I didn't want to be wrong.

"Where are we going?" I asked.

"We are going that way." He pointed to another trail and then began to walk. I followed, trying to resist the urge to sprint back to my family. If my suspicion was right I needed to trust this guy. We walked away from the meadow and my heart ached; everything in me wanted to turn around.

The trail wound back and forth and the forest got dense. Giant ferns sprung up from the ground and the life of the wilderness was everywhere. A deer skittishly shot away as we approached, bunnies ran back and forth, bark was stripped back on the trees from clawing bears and the sun's rays peaked through the open holes in the foliage.

The trail widened and opened up into a large dirt covered clearing. In the middle of this clearing was a small burning campfire encircled by several tree stumps. The man approached the circle and sat down; he motioned for me to sit down as well. I sat down on the stump next to him and waited. *Why were we here? What was next? Was he who I thought he was?* He stoked the fire with a stick and then turned his body towards me.

"Ask me my child. I will answer," he said softly. I felt the significance of the moment. If he was who I thought he was, this conversation would be the most important one of my life.

"Are you Jesus?" I asked and my heart skipped a beat.

"If that is what you wish to call me…I am who I am," He answered.

"So are you God?" I asked again, trying to remember my theology and my understanding of Christ, the Trinity…it was all really confusing.

"People have given me many names. Many religions have formed as you try to understand. People have said and written many things about me in many different forms, languages and books. Some true, some lies, some a bit of both. Everything you have heard about me from man is exactly that, but what you feel on your heart about me…that is who I am." He answered and I tried to understand.

"So, you are what exactly?" I wanted a definition.

"I am," He smiled and placed his hand on my knee. "I am. Trust me."

"How can I trust something I don't understand?" I asked.

"You do, David…you just have to listen," He replied, "I am in your heart, if you listen you will find me. I am creation. I am in your soul. I am. Free your heart…it will tell you."

Immediately my mind reminded me of all the contradictions of the god I learned about. How could evil exist? Why was the god of the Bible so cruel? If He was all powerful

81

and all good, how could he explain all the bad things? Bad things like people dying in car crashes, things like cancer, and really evil things like the holocaust. If I was sitting here with the divine creator he had some explaining to do.

"Why, then, do bad things happen? Creation isn't always beautiful." I asked the question not as a judgment but with hope. Hope that He was all He claimed to be.

"Your fish was bloody and now she is swimming. Your family is together right now as we speak; your voice is back and able to ask such thoughtful questions. I make all things new. I erase all pain and I make all things good. I am salvation, I am hope. No evil or pain can escape my love. All who are lost will be found...all who suffer will place their burdens on me." He answered.

"But why pain in the first place?" I asked. "And why can't you intervene to stop bad things?"

"I have and I am," He answered, "not all is as it seems..."

His answer didn't seem totally acceptable. People obviously die and suffer. I saw no intervention when my parents moaned in pain as they died. Obviously things were better for me now, but what about those who never have this experience? Or what about those who never find God? Would an atheist holocaust survivor accept this answer?

"I created this," He raised his arms to signify everything around us. "I will never abandon my children...as a mother experiences labor to receive the gift of her child, my creation has to grow too before it will accept me. I am always ready but sometimes you are not...and sometimes the journey hurts...but that is not my choice, it is yours."

"Well can't you make it hurt less?" I asked.

"That is up to you," He answered.

"But I don't have that kind of power," I replied.

"You all do. You all have my love in your hearts...this is a power greater than all of creation...I created you this way, in my image. It is my greatest gift to you."

I had a feeling that I was never going to fully understand what he was talking about, but his answers sure seemed a lot better than anything I was ever taught in church. I decided to continue with questions, most created from my church going days.

"So, what about those who never find you?" I asked. I wanted to explore my really big question, the concept of an eternal hell, the notion that entire civilizations who believe in a different system of salvation all suffer because they were wrong. I found this completely contradictory with an all-loving god. Hell, as I understood it, presented a moral flaw in the god of religion.

"Trust me." His look became very serious, and then He spoke very slowly to emphasize the point, "I will never abandon my children, not in this life or the next."

"But."

He cut me off, "But nothing! There are no exceptions. You are ALL my children...which is why you are here today."

"You mean so you can answer my questions? So I can be found?" I replied.

"Actually," He smiled, "this isn't just about you. Your family has already healed your heart...you have been found. "

"Huh?"

"This moment is about a different man who needs to heal. A man who needs my love, who needs to come home," He said.

"So, what does that have to do with me?" I asked.

"His name is Brian," he continued, not answering my question.

"Brian...is this the same Brian that my sister was talking about?"

"Yes." He paused. "Seeing Brian will be difficult for you."

"Why?" My mind raced trying to understand what He was conveying.

"Because, he lived a life of sadness...his life on earth was hell. His parents never loved him; he became addicted to alcohol. He never listened to his heart." He stopped as if to collect himself from crying and then he continued. "As a man he was a drunk. He hurt those around him and he ended his life as a murderer."

"And you love him?" I asked.

"With all my heart," He replied.

"Why do I need to meet him?" I asked.

"Because he was the driver of the car. He was the one who killed your family."

To forgive is to set a prisoner free and to discover that the prisoner was you.
~Lewis B. Smedes

Chapter Twelve

Brian McDaniels! I remembered the man's full name. My only escape a few months back had been to fantasize about destroying this man, just as he had destroyed me. Now, here in this strange world, he was friends with my sister. *Why does this man get redemption?* I thought. *He doesn't deserve it!* My heart began to pump and I could feel the adrenaline of rage beginning to surface. My hatred was still alive in me.

"What we are entitled to has nothing to do with my love, Son." It was obvious He could read my thoughts. "Hate only brings darkness and destruction."

He was right but I couldn't shake the feeling. My body began to perspire. I didn't want to meet this man.

"Close your eyes," He instructed and I obeyed. "Now, just listen."

I took a few deep breaths and tried to calm myself. I felt Him come closer and he put His arms around me. My body instantly became relaxed and full of peace. My breathing slowed down to a more relaxed pace. With my eyes closed I saw my family in the meadow. I heard my sister laughing and my parents talking. I listened more and I saw the Madison River, I saw my grandfather and father passing by in a drift boat. I listened even more as I felt His presence.

"What do you hear, Son?" He asked.

"Forgive," I answered.

"Good. Open your eyes." He released His hug and backed away.

I opened my eyes and in the distance I saw another man. He was just standing there, staring at us, about twenty feet away. He looked like he was in his thirties, balding and a little overweight. His attire was simple, some white sneakers, jeans and a grey hooded sweatshirt. He looked terrified.

"Come, Brian," He said. The man listened and walked towards us. As he got closer, I could tell that he was shaking. When he was only a few steps away he was trembling so badly that he could barely walk. Then he fell to the ground, right in front of me.

"Oh, I am so sorry," he cried. His body convulsed and loud sobs followed. "I never meant to hurt anyone."

I turned to look at God for what to do, but He was gone. I was all alone now in the woods with the murderer of my family begging for mercy. His head was touching my feet and my hand moved out. At first my hand was shaking and I made a fist, wanting to inflict pain. Then I gained control, my hand gently opened and rested on his head.

"Don't cry," I said. "Everything is okay now. You are home, Brian." Never before had I felt such power in my words. This was the greatest moment my voice had ever had. My body never felt so pure. I was in rhythm with my heart and soul…I released my hate.

Brian looked up from the ground then moved to his feet; he threw his arms around me and I responded by throwing mine around him. He kept sobbing and I kept holding him.

"I really love your family," he said through the sobs. "Your sister is my best friend…I don't know what I would do without her."

I didn't really understand how they were friends or how he knew my family. My mind couldn't grasp who God really was, what this place was, why I was here, or why I was needed for this moment in Brian's redemption. All I could understand was that God was good and that I could trust Him.

"I'm glad you like them, Brian," I responded, "I like them, too."

"Maybe when you get here we can all hang out?" he asked.

"You know…I would like that." I smiled.

Sing for joy, O heavens, for the LORD has done this; shout aloud, O earth beneath. Burst into song, you mountains, you forests and all your trees, for the LORD has redeemed Jacob, he displays his glory in Israel.
~ Isaiah 44:23

Chapter Thirteen

"Brian! Big Brother!" The happy screams of a little girl ended my isolated time with Brian. Running down the trail which led to our campfire was my sister. Brian ran to meet her and she jumped into his arms.

"Hey, sweetie, I missed you," he said softly as he kissed her forehead.

"Did he forgive you?" She pointed to me.

"Yes, he did," Brian smiled as he looked at me. "He reminds me of Moose." Brian couldn't have paid me a better compliment.

"Good," she said as Brian put her down. Once her feet hit the ground she took two steps and then leaped into my arms. "Now we can sing!" she exclaimed with joy and anticipation.

Just then I noticed more figures making their way down the trail and towards our location. It was my dad with a guitar under one arm and my mom under the other. My sister wiggled out of my arms and ran to meet them.

"Mom! Dad!" I rejoiced and greeted them with big long hugs. The joy which ran through my body was indescribable. *My family is reunited,* I thought. I wanted to start talking, we had so much to say…but before I could begin my dad was strumming chords on the guitar, and before I realized what was forming everyone was already in rhythm. Around the campfire, they all found a seat as the words of *Here I am to Worship* echoed from the lungs of the group against the forest walls.

Here I am to Worship
Here I am to Bow Down, Here I am to say that you're my God
You're all together lovely, all together worthy, all together wonderful
to me

I knew the words well as I had heard them many times before in church. I remembered my aunt listening to this song as she drove me to Ennis. I wondered how she was holding up. Last time I saw her it wasn't good and I wanted to share this feeling with her. The music was more beautiful than any I had ever heard; conversations could wait.

After *Here I am to Worship*, my dad quickly transitioned his strumming to the chords of *God of Wonders*. This was my favorite worship song of all time and I joined in singing...

God of Wonders beyond our galaxy...you are holy...holy
The universe declares your majesty
Precious Lord Reveal your heart me, you are holy, oh father holy...

My dad was sitting on the stump to my left, his eyes closed as he strummed away, deep in worship. My mother sat to the right of me, with my sister in her lap and Brian directly across, all singing with complete passion and no shame. Their hearts were naked and free and the moment consumed my being.

Some of the songs I recognized. Others, I had never heard. When we sang *Imagine*, by John Lennon, at first it didn't seem to fit. But as I listened, the words of this secular song described these woods so perfectly.

Imagine there's no countries, it's not that hard to do
Nothing to kill or die for, and no religion too
Imagine all the people, living life in peace

You may say I'm a dreamer, but I'm not the only one
I hope someday you will join us, and the world will be as one

95

I wondered if God put this song in Lennon's heart. Considering this moment, I had to suspect that he did. It was then that I really connected what He was saying. God isn't a religion, a book, or any man-made thing that tries to attach itself to Him. Muslims, Christians or any other group, person or book that claims to have the market on God isn't listening to Him. God is simply God, we only need to listen to our hearts to find Him. *A free heart finds God,* I thought.

In the distance I saw Him. He was talking with a couple other figures as they watched our makeshift worship session. I wondered who the other two were. *Were they angels? Other people? The Trinity?* I leaned over to my mom as she sang.

"Who are they?" I whispered in her ear.

"Your father and I will explain it to you one day dear…in the meadow," she turned back and then kissed my cheek. "He is good and He is love David…nothing else matters." She was right and her answer was completely acceptable to me.

The forest started to get dark and Brian got up and built the fire to a roar. The flames and sparks from the heat shot up towards the sky. As the fire crackled and the music continued, I looked up to the night. Stars and planets were beginning to appear and several shooting stars made their way across the tapestry. *God of Wonders,* I thought. Then I felt Him tapping on my shoulder.

"It is time, son," He spoke. "Time to go back."

I was so warm and content sitting by the fire with my family, nothing in me ever wanted to leave. But today had taught me many things, and now I knew I could trust His wisdom and direction.

"Okay, God," I replied and stood up. My family didn't stop singing but they all waved and smiled. My sister blew me a big kiss with her hand and then I turned to walk away with my trusted friend.

We wound down another trail which I hadn't noticed before. The path quickly turned from forest to tall grass; I soon realized we were back in the Madison Valley. The trail and our steps brought us back to the rock, the rock where I met Moose and where this fantastic adventure all began. He stopped and turned towards me.

"Are you ready to return to earth, Son?" He asked.

"Will I ever see them again?" I questioned, scared of returning to a life without.

"No." The words stung my heart.

"But…I can't live without them."

"Just because you can't see them doesn't mean you will be without them…listen to your heart, Son…they will always be there." His voice was so strong and caring.

"How about you…will I get to see you?" I started to cry.

"I am everywhere, Son…your heart will always see me," He promised. "Just remember that one day I will bring you all home."

"Promise?" I said through my tears.

"Yes, I promise…and one day you will bring your own family to the meadow."

"You mean I am going to have children of my own?" I had never really thought about the possibility. I guess I was too stuck in my own misery to think about the future. Having a family of my own sounded really nice. I wanted to be a good father just like my dad was for me.

"You are going to be a great dad, David," He replied. "But, first you need to take care of Sarah." I knew who He meant.

"You mean my aunt?" I asked for verification.

"Yes," He looked at me with seriousness. "It is your turn now…help her through her sadness."

"Her marriage?" I figured she was probably getting divorced.

"Yes, and the loss of her mother," he answered.

"Grandma!"

He gave a look of reassurance and peace, I understood.

"Listen to your heart, Son, you know the story now...your heart is free; have the courage to follow it." He then kissed me on the forehead and began to walk away. In his kiss I felt, no I saw...I saw everything. The Madison flowing in the sun, my little sister hugging my neck, my parents full of love in the meadow and a giant trout running free, free from the wounds and blood this world can bring. Simply put, He showed me love. He revealed His plan. He freed my heart.

My body froze as he began to leave. My legs and my heart just wanted to follow him back...back to the campfire, the meadow...back to heaven. It was then that I noticed that his feet were no longer on solid ground. He was moving gracefully over the Madison, walking on water. My eyes fixated on the wonder of this Being. He stopped halfway over the river to turn and offer his final words to me.

"You are quite a fisherman, Son...now be a fisher of men," His words bellowed over the water. Then I watched Him walk away and disappear into the evening mist. Not out of my life but into it.

Don't cry because it is over. Smile because it happened.
~Dr. Seuss

Chapter Fourteen

As I walked back to Grandma's house, I didn't know
what to expect. I knew from my talk with God that she didn't
have much time. I wondered how I would handle it and if I
could be strong enough for my aunt. For the first time in a really
long time, I prayed. I asked for strength and comfort and I
asked for guidance and wisdom; most of all I thanked God for
rescuing and loving me. With my heart now free, I heard Him.
It was almost like a conversation without words and voices...I
had heard people talk about this experience of prayer and I had
always dismissed them as crazy...I now knew I was the crazy
one. He was right that He would never leave me.

A police car marked, *Montana State Patrol,* was waiting for
me as I approached the house. It sat there in the darkness,
engine on and idling, just waiting. I had a bad feeling about what
this meant. As I approached the officer sitting the car noticed
and turned the engine off. He got out of the vehicle, closed the
car door and started walking to meet me.

"David...David Tucker?" He called my name as I
approached. He was tall, slender and didn't look much older
than me.

"That's me!" I shouted back as I closed in the final ten or
so yards between us.

"You sure?" he asked.

"Yeah, that's me," I responded cautiously. We were now
standing face to face by the side of my grandma's house.

"Oh, it's just that I heard you couldn't talk," he answered.

102

"Yeah, I just started talking again about a day ago...what's this all about?" I asked and I felt my stomach tighten, ready to brace for the bad news.

"It's your grandma," he said. I could tell that he was really nervous and his face and body language suggested that he just wanted to run away.

"Is she ok?" I asked.

"She had a stroke today...when she was at the grocery store," he answered.

"Where is she?"

"She's in Bozeman at a really good hospital. I was told to wait for you...I can give you a ride there now," he offered.

"Yes. Let's go!" I began moving towards the car.

We both quickly got in and fastened our seat belts. The officer backed the patrol car out and then hit the lights. We were out of Ennis and on the highway in a matter of seconds. Voices over his radio came in and out, speaking a language of code words that was very unfamiliar to me.

"We should be in Bozeman in no time, David," the officer told me. "And your aunt...Sarah...your grandma had her listed as a contact...she is driving to Bozeman right now as well...so however long that takes she should be here soon."

"About twelve hours," I informed the officer.

"Okay good...well we should be to the hospital in less than thirty minutes," and that ended our conversation. We both sat quietly listening to the highway patrol as we sped our way to Bozeman.

When we got there, the officer walked me inside and then introduced me to a Ms. Fink. After that the officer left and I was alone in a very foreign environment.

"Can I get you anything, David?" Ms. Fink asked. She was older, probably in her late fifties. She had short, brown curly hair and was wearing a professional blue suit. "Water, juice...something to eat?"

"When can I see my grandma?" I ignored her question.

"Really soon," she answered.

103

"Are you a doctor?" I questioned, wondering who this lady and why the officer left me in her custody.

"I'm a social worker for the hospital," she said.

"What does that mean?"

"It means I am here to help." She smiled. "When your aunt gets here, she can take over but for now I will have to do."

I nodded. *She seems nice enough*, I thought.

Just then a few nurses rushed up to Ms. Fink and pulled her aside.

"Just a second, David," she told me as she took a few steps and then engaged into what appeared to be a serious discussion with the other nurses. The conversation was quick and she then walked back over to me.

"David, your grandma is dying; follow me and you can say goodbye," she said so matter of fact. I followed without hesitation.

We entered through two big double doors and then made a few turns down a series of long hallways. Then Ms. Fink stopped in front and pointed to an open door. Out of that door walked a nurse.

"Is this him?" the nurse asked.

"Yes," Ms. Fink replied.

"Ok, David, go on in. You don't have much time," she said.

My legs moved me into the room and I walked past the half-drawn ceiling curtain towards the bed which held my grandma. Next to her bed were a few beeping machines and several tubes were in her arms. I walked closer and stood at the side of the bed, looking directly down at her. Her body looked so worn and weathered, so different than the person I shared scotch with the night before. She was barely breathing and the smell of death stuffed the room.

"Hey, Grandma," I said, hoping she could hear me.

Her eyes opened and her hand moved slightly. I placed my hand in hers and her fingers closed around mine. Her mouth tried to move and she started whispering. I couldn't make out the words.

"Yes, Grandma," I said back. "I can hear you."

"It's beautiful," she voiced loud and clear and then closed her eyes. I kept holding her hand and I felt her life fade away. I bent over and gave her a kiss on the forehead. The machine behind me wasn't beeping anymore.

"Goodbye…" I whispered. "See you soon."

You were born with potential
You were born with goodness and trust
You were born with ideals, You were born with dreams
You were born with greatness, You were born with wings
You are not meant for crawling, so don't
You have wings, learn to use them and fly
~Rumi

Chapter Fifteen

The auditorium at Bellingham High School was packed. It was summertime and the stands were filled with people of all ages, people who all had experienced pain in their lives and people who were looking to live and love again. Today marked the end of the *FreeHeart* convention, and this was the moment of my closing speech. Even though I had spoken to many crowds like this, today was special. I turned to give my beautiful wife, Ashley, a kiss and our five year old daughter, Ali, a hug. I walked out to the applause.

"Good afternoon," I began.

"Good afternoon," they echoed back. Even though I was now in my late-thirties I still felt like that sixteen-year-old boy who discovered a world of love so many years ago. My career as a social worker and psychologist had aged me but my spirit felt the same. My latest book, *FreeHeart,* was a bestseller and had allowed me to play a part in the journey and healing of so many. Before I continued, I closed my eyes and thanked God. I thanked him for this moment, my family, and the wonder of life. I was truly blessed.

I began my closing speech and I could feel Him by my side.

"You know I attended this high school. It was only for a few months and during the worst time of my life. It was so bad that I couldn't talk. I just couldn't handle the loss, the pain, the defeat. I had lost my entire family in a senseless car wreck. My dad, my mom and my

108

sister...and in that loss, I also lost myself. I was alone and afraid. I had no hope and I was lost in the darkness.

Many of you, right now, are feeling that same pain. You are not alone. Today, I met with a family who lost their youngest son to cancer. I spoke with a husband who just lost his wife. I heard the story of a mother dealing with the sorrow of miscarriage. I cried with a young man who lost his best friend to suicide. Your stories are so painful, and in many ways they are something that no one can truly understand, but we all share the journey in our own unique way. I am not here to patronize your loss or to over simplify matters by simply saying get over it or that it is all part of God's plan. Your mourning and your sadness are justified and well deserved...but I am here to tell you that there is something else beyond all the hurt and loss...and in time you will receive it. We all will.

I paused and looked out to the audience. Sometimes, during these moments, I swear I can see them. Today, I didn't see Moose or anyone else, but I felt them. I continued.

"Listen to your heart and you will feel it. Listen and you will hear God.

The circumstances of life can make living difficult. Loss, rejection, and heartbreak prevent us from hearing. Politics and religion, they suffocate us. And the greatest blockade of all...fear. Fear is behind all of our actions which take us away from life. Fear plugs our ears so tight that we can no longer hear. We go through life fearing loss, fearing death, fearing hell. We need to let go...fear does not belong.

I am saying to you today...mourn, cry and honor those you have lost. But do not fear. Do not lose heart. Take your wounds and allow them to heal. Then listen...and you will hear them.

Nothing in our existence is guaranteed. Each day that we have is a gift. But there is one guarantee beyond all of this. That guarantee is love. Free your heart and join me...join us...join us in honoring those we have lost by living a life that honors them."

I walked away from the podium and back towards my family. The applause of the crowd filled the stuffy auditorium. Silently, I prayed that my voice could help those clapping hands which so generously acknowledged my closing remarks.

109

My daughter jumped into my arms and a gym manager guided my wife and me past the crowds and out the back entrance. Once outside we headed over to our family truck. The pickup's bed was loaded with gear: tents, coolers, fishing supplies and all the necessities for camping. Today marked the end of my book tour and the beginning of our summer vacation. I had spent so much time the last few years helping others that this alone time with my family was well deserved and much needed.

We were giddy with excitement as we boarded the truck and headed out of town. Ali was bouncing up and down in her seat with excitement and Ashley turned around to inspect the contents of a few bags, double checking that everything was in order.

When I merged onto the highway she looked at me and placed her hand on my leg.

"Good job today, baby," she affirmed.

"You think? Sometimes I just worry that I can't help...that words don't mean much."

"They all need to find their own way baby, that is not your responsibility...and, I heard your words and I watched the way you connected with those people. You *are* helping." Her voice always so loving and perfect.

"Hey, Daddy?" my little girl interrupted.

"Yes, Ali," I answered.

"When are we going to see Grandma Tucker?" My aunt Sarah had become my "mom" and as far as my daughter knew she was grandma. A loving, wonderful grandma, just like the one I had as a child.

"When we get there, Sweetie. We have a long drive ahead of us," I called back.

My aunt and I spent several years together in Ennis after the passing of my grandma and the ending of my aunt's marriage. Eventually, I came back to Seattle for college, but my aunt never left and I was glad about that. My aunt's wounds healed alongside that same river which healed my heart. It was her home.

"Why is Ennis so far away?" Ali shot back.

My daughter loved Ennis. She loved our ritual of hanging out with Grandma and then camping at Jack Creek. My wife and I were committed to making annual trips to our family location, and the joy it brought to my daughter and to us was well worth the long drive.

I looked in my rearview mirror at Ali. She was wearing a little yellow summer dress and her hair was pulled into two cute, blond pig-tails. She reminded me so much of another girl I once met.

"Because sometimes we have to be patient before we can get to where God wants us to be." My answer seemed to be acceptable to her for now.

"I love you, Daddy," she said.

"I love you too, Sweetie…I love you so much."

We headed down the interstate and towards our next journey together. Our hearts were free.

www.ingramcontent.com/pod-product-compliance
Lightning Source LLC
Chambersburg PA
CBHW070603180626
46817CB00005B/1974